The Prince Who Was Just Himself

The Prince Who Was Just Himself

Silke Schnee

Illustrations by Heike Sistig

Translated by Erna Albertz

Plough Publishing House

Published by Plough Publishing House
Walden, New York
Robertsbridge, England
Elsmore, Australia
www.plough.com

The German original edition of this book has been published under the
title *Die Geschichte von Prinz Seltsam* by Neufeld Verlag, Schwarzenfeld, Germany.
Copyright © 2011 Neufeld Verlag. All rights reserved.

Illustrated by Heike Sistig
Translated from the German by Erna Albertz

ISBN: 978-0-87486-682-7
20 19 18 17 16 15   1 2 3 4 5 6

Library of Congress Cataloging-in-Publication Data pending.

Printed in Mexico

Once upon a time there lived a king and a queen who had two sons: big Prince Luke and little Prince Jonas.

"Two children are not enough for me," said the queen to the king one day. "I wish we had more children. Children are simply wonderful!"

The king was not so sure. He looked at all the castle windows that had been cracked during princely soccer games. He remembered the princes' howls of protest when they didn't want to go to bed in the evening.

He felt tiredness creep over him as he thought of being awakened every night by the princes who wanted to sleep close to him in his big, kingly bed.

But the queen took the king by the arm and led him down into the palace gardens. There before their very eyes Prince Jonas made a perfect penalty kick.

The king was mighty proud of him.

After the usual bedtime howls, he tucked the princes into bed. Then Prince Luke read aloud to him from his favorite book.

The king's heart was softened and he was mighty proud of his older son.

In the middle of the night when two little princes crept into the royal bed, the king moved over to make room for them and thought, "There's nothing more wonderful in the world than having children."

One day the queen announced that she was expecting a baby, and everyone was terribly excited. After many months of waiting, Prince Noah was born.

"He looks a little different," said the king.
"He is not like the others," agreed the queen.
"He is our brother," said Prince Luke.
"He is just himself," said Prince Jonas.

And right away, they all loved Prince Noah very, very much.

When the royal family proudly presented Prince Noah to the people, they were quite surprised. A few of them whispered behind their hands to each other, "What an unusual prince." Some began to laugh, while others were downright mean and shouted, "He is not one of us!"

The Prince Who Was Just Himself only smiled at them and was happy to be out in the sun. He did everything very slowly, just like someone who takes his time doing something he loves because he wants to enjoy every minute of it.

He crawled unhurriedly across the royal lawn, stopping to look carefully at every daisy he came across.

He listened quietly and thoughtfully whenever the queen sang to him, and he never interrupted her.

He was not very good at running and jumping, but it didn't matter because he was never in a hurry anyhow. He liked being wherever he was and was not worried about where he would go next.

He hardly ever used words or sentences, yet people understood him just as well.

One day a great storm arose and the sun was darkened. The terrible knight Scarface wanted to attack the kingdom.

The royal family and all the people of the land were terrified. But the princes knew they had to protect their kingdom, so the three of them saddled their horses and rode out onto the battlefield.

The great knight Scarface looked wicked and powerful. He sat bolt upright upon his horse and raised his sword above his head. His mighty army was assembled behind him, waiting only for him to give the signal to attack by letting his sword come crashing down.

All the warriors held their breath. Only the storm-wind blew in gusts that made their armor creak and rattle.

Scarface braced himself against the gusts and angrily raised his head still higher so that he would look even bigger and fiercer. The wind made his eyes water, and tears ran down his cheeks in little streams.

At this, the Prince Who Was Just Himself cocked his head and looked intently at the knight. Suddenly, without saying a word – as was his custom – he spurred on his horse, and rode directly toward Scarface, stopping only when he was right in front of him. Then Prince Noah stretched out his little right hand and touched the scar on the knight's face. Looking deeply into his tear-filled eyes he asked in a soft, caring voice, "Does it hurt?"

Scarface opened his mouth and then shut it again. Bewildered, he let his sword arm sink to his side. He shook himself and rubbed his eyes in surprise. He stared at Prince Noah, whose little hand was still touching the scar on his face.

Such a thing had never happened to Scarface before. He knew all about hate and fighting. But he had never before encountered love and caring. Strange new feelings filled his heart, and he didn't know what to do.

He began to tremble all over. First his teeth chattered, then his armor rattled, and then even the legs of his horse began to shake.

In order to warm him, the Prince Who Was Just Himself threw his arms around the mighty Scarface.

A hush fell over everyone. Even the storm quieted down and the sun peeked out from behind a cloud, not wanting to miss what was happening. As they watched, a smile slowly spread across the knight's face.

And then a voice broke the silence, "Long live Prince Noah! He has saved us! Long may he live!" More and more voices joined the chorus, sounding louder and happier every moment, "Long live Prince Noah! Our great Prince Noah!"

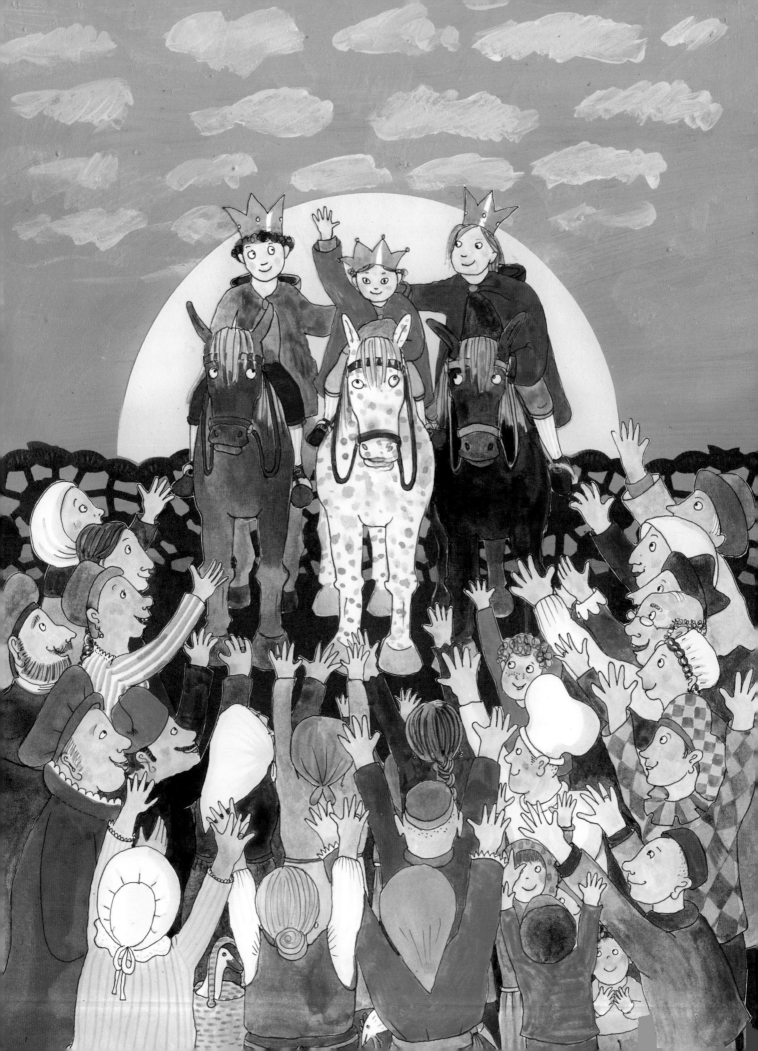

The king and the queen, Prince Luke and Prince Jonas, and all the people of the land were mighty proud of the little prince.

The Prince Who Was Just Himself only smiled at them and was happy to be out in the sun.

The Author

Silke Schnee is a journalist and works as a television producer for a public broadcaster in Cologne, Germany. She is married and has three

sons. Her youngest son Noah was born in July 2008 with Trisomy 21 (Down syndrome). She writes, "At first when Noah was born, we were shocked and sad. The catalyst for this book was witnessing

the effect he had on many people, despite being categorized as disabled. In fact, our little prince brings much love, joy, and sunshine not only

to us, but to all around him. Children are a wonder, and we must see them with the eyes of our heart – each child just the way he or she is."

Bild: © WDR

The Illustrator

Heike Sistig studied special education and art and is a trained art therapist. She works as an editor for children's television programming.

She has illustrated several children's books, and has exhibited her collages in several galleries. She lives with her family in Cologne, Germany.

What is Down syndrome?

One in every 691 babies in the United States is born with Down syndrome, making it the most frequently occurring chromosomal condition. People with Down syndrome have 47 instead of the usual 46 chromosomes in their genetic makeup: they possess an extra copy of the 21st chromosome, which is why Down syndrome is also known as trisomy 21. Down syndrome is a permanent condition, and causes mild to moderate delays in physical and intellectual development.

There are people with Down syndrome all over the world, in every ethnic group, country, and class. The condition is characterized by small stature, low muscle tone, an upward slant to the eyes, and a single crease across the center of the palm. However, not everyone with Down syndrome possesses all of these characteristics. Evidence of individuals with Down syndrome has been found in ancient art, literature, and science. In 1866, John Langdon Down, a British physician, first described the condition as a distinct and separate entity; the syndrome was named after him as a result.

Due to advances in medical care, most individuals with Down syndrome will reach their sixtieth birthday. They have become increasingly integrated into the communities and societies they live in. People with Down syndrome have many talents; several are well known as actors and actresses, artists, and Special Olympians. Some are able to hold jobs and live independently, and many live and work with minimal assistance. All of this contributes to a better outlook today for people living with Down syndrome than ever before.

According to a recent study, 99 percent of people with Down syndrome say they are happy with their lives, and 94 percent of siblings of individuals with Down syndrome reported that they are proud of their sibling. The most important fact to know about people with Down syndrome is that they are more like others than they are different. They are capable of living happy and purposeful lives.

(adapted from the sources listed below)

The following organizations can provide further information on Down syndrome:

National Down Syndrome Society (NDSS)

National Association for Down Syndrome (NADS)

National Down Syndrome Congress (NDSC)

Their Name Is Today

Reclaiming Childhood in a Hostile World

Johann Christoph Arnold

Foreword by
Mark K. Shriver
192 pages, softcover

Because every child learns differently . . .

When it comes to raising and teaching children, one size doesn't fit all. That's what excites Johann Christoph Arnold, whose books on education, parenting, and relationships have helped more than a million readers through life's challenges.

Despite a perfect storm of forces that threaten children's individuality, Arnold assures parents and teachers that they actually know what's best for each child. Through real-life stories, he explores the effects of technology, standardized testing, overstimulation, academic pressure, marketing to children, over-diagnosis and much more, calling on everyone who loves children to combat these threats to childhood and find creative ways to help each child flourish.

Diane Komp, MD, Professor of Pediatrics, Yale University
Stunning. . . . Who would have thought that there was anything new to say about childhood? Arnold surprises us at every turn.

Jonathan Kozol, author
Beautiful. . . . It is Arnold's reverence for children that I love.

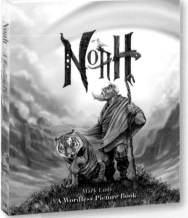

Noah
A Wordless
Picture Book

Mark Ludy
64 pages, hardcover

*Bonus: Find Squeakers
the mouse on every page.*

Who needs text to tell a story?

A hundred years before the Great Flood, a man named Noah came home talking crazy. God wanted him to build the biggest ship the world had ever seen. How would his wife respond? What would the neighbors think?

This lavish reimagining of one of the greatest stories of all time will fascinate children and adults alike. Nuanced and playful, Mark Ludy's world-class art digs deeper than the Sunday-school tale of cuddly animals, exploring Noah's relationship with his family, the natural world, God – and a formidable engineering challenge.

Penny Ray, mother of a child with autism
Ludy's images tell the story and more; they are colorful, visually descriptive – simply stunning! Sometimes, text can be an obstacle to comprehension: the young reader is so focused on decoding words that there is no room for meaning. A wordless book allows us to concentrate on the story itself. My daughter and I can hold the book together and describe something each of us notices on every page. I learn a lot about her by what she sees.

Plough Publishing House, www.plough.com, 1-800-521-8011
151 Bowne Drive, PO Box 398, Walden, NY 12586, USA
Brightling Rd, Robertsbridge, East Sussex TN32 5DR, UK
4188 Gwydir Highway, Elsmore, NSW 2360, AU